THE VAMPIRE CLAN

THE VAMPIRE CLAN

THE TAKING OF FINNEGAN

PART 1

MICHAEL VETO

Michael Veto
The Vampire Clan

All rights reserved
Copyright © 2024 by Michael Veto

No part of this publication may be reproduced, distributed, or transmitted in any form or by any means, including photocopying, recording, or other electronic or mechanical methods, without the prior written permission of the publisher, except in the case of brief quotations embodied in critical reviews and certain other noncommercial uses permitted by copyright law.

This book is a work of fiction, all characters depicted in this book are fictitious, and any resemblance to real people, living or dead, is purely coincidental.

Published by Spines
ISBN 979-8-89569-776-4

Contents

Introduction

When I wrote Finnegan back in 2017, I was rushing it. The reason I was rushing it is because after I wrote The Dark Entity.

When I first wrote Finnegan, I wrote it originally as a children's book, but I had friends who read it, and they felt it would be too dramatizing for them to understand. You will notice multiple copies, as I was trying to publish it myself. The issue is that this story is too short to publish.

This version is going to be longer. I don't want this story to be stuck in a series. When it comes to that, we will see how this one goes. I'm excited about this to see where this will land and how Finnegan will do under pressure.

But I was thinking about why people would want this dog, and there is a neat twist to this. I'm also changing the title of the book.

I am making this version more eerie than the other versions, and yes, this would not be for a child to read; this will be geared towards adults.

I even added a whole new take on the original book. It will be more morbid than the last few versions and I'm excited about this. I have never written anything like this before, so we are in it together. So welcome to the adventure. The new title is called The Vampire Clan.

I know I said at the beginning of this introduction that I wasn't going to write any sequels, but to tell this whole story, I'm going to set it up so that it can continue. I'm sorry to disappoint some folks, but the whole story has undergone a huge change, which happens from time to time. I really hope you enjoy reading it because I enjoyed writing and more to come.

-MV

CHAPTER 1

Finnegan was my favorite pet. She was adorable at times, and if I was in a bad mood, she was always there to cheer me up.

Let me tell you a little about Finnegan. In fact, this is her story, not mine. I promise you there will be a lot of happiness; some tears may come down your cheeks as I am telling this story.

Mostly happiness and there are a lot of adventures if that is what you are looking for. So here we go. We know that dogs and animals do not talk. But in my story, Finnegan talks like humans do.

Finnegan was born on March 12, 1976. She was born as a beautiful puppy. Finnegan was growing at a rapid pace. She was bigger than a one-year-old puppy should be. Even though parents will be in bookstores and spend a lot of time in the library, in the library children's section, I knew they would come across my books, and they would get drawn in by just looking at the cover, authoring these books, and seeing the joy of their children gives me bundles of joy.

There was a time that I was in the library, and I saw some

kids looking at my books, and they were so amazed at how well my book cover looked; they were drawn in. On with the story, I really do not have a lot of time to write this. I only have so many pages to get this on.

The house was a yellow Colonial that had two floors. The kitchen was on the second floor. The outside, on the left side of the house, was a set of stairs. They were stained brown, they led up to the door to the kitchen, there were twelve steps, and the back of the house was a deck, so we could have parties and cookouts of that nature.

So, like I said, I only live about ten minutes away from the animal shelter. I got into my 1957 Chevy Bel-Air Coupe. It was blue, like the color of the sky. The car was handed down to me when my mother died from lung cancer five years ago. Then, two years ago, my father passed away and left me the house. He died from a broken heart.

The back of the house and the backyard had a lot of room, and there was grass and gravel, which was covered with snow. The yard was surrounded by a stained brown shed where I kept lawnmowers, rakes, shovels for digging dirt and shoveling snow, soccer balls, and basketballs. On the left side of the shed is a wooden fence that starts at the beginning of my backyard and goes all the way down past the fence. It divides the two property lines. Before the grass, there are three rows of gravel, and there is more gravel underneath the deck. But everything is covered with snow and ice. We got a bad snow and ice storm not too long ago.

The house sits in the middle of the property. The house is yellow-sided, meaning my father did not paint it. It would have been too much work to paint it every year, and I was afraid of heights. So, I did not go on ladders. There was grass in the front and to the right side but visible in front of the property is a big granny apple tree. My father wanted to cut it down, but he did not. He could not take the tree down because it was too costly to have done; the branches were too long, and they were about touching the power lines.

In front of the lawn is a small wooden fence, and before the fence is a large area for gravel. This gravel was incredible to my father. He never allowed people to park on the gravel. The last thing I would like to describe to you is the driveway.

The driveway had a strange design. It was made into an L shape design so it would be able to fit three cars. So, it was long. It started from the gravel and the mailbox and went to the fence. The way it would fit two cars. The other parking space was not as big; it was only big enough to fit one car, and at the end of it, it had an adjustable basketball hoop. My older brother and I used to love playing basketball, especially in the dark.

So, I got a phone call from the animal shelter that called me about adopting a dog. They thought I might be interested in seeing and adopting a new one, so I came out of my house, and I got into my car. Back in those days, we didn't have to lock our doors.

So, I got into my car. I had a black winter jacket on, some warm gloves, and a large black warm winter hat to keep my head and ears warm. I am slim, six feet tall, and people do not understand why I do not have kids yet or with anyone, but I needed to get to the animal shelter quickly. I started up the car, and on the first shot, she purred like a kitten. I turned the heat on, and I waited for a few minutes, I needed to wait until the car warmed up.

Five minutes later, the car was getting warm, and the windows were getting warm; the windows were not fogged and iced up. Otherwise, not frozen. Therefore, I love this car; it never gives me a tough time, and it treats me well. That is because I treat her well.

I put the car in reverse, and I looked to make sure there were no cars coming, which there would not be because this street is not busy with traffic. I went ahead to back up. Once I backed out of the driveway, I put the car in drive to the right and drove up Nelson Street.

It was cold out, but the sky was blue, the sun was shining, and unbelievably, there was not a cloud in the sky. As I was driving up Nelson Street, I saw the neighbors outside putting salt and sand on their driveways and sidewalks. They all knew me because of the books I had written. They all like my car; the reason I know this is because when I honk the horn and wave, they all shout out. "Love the car." I often get a thumbs-up.

When I am driving in the car, I do not like having the radio on because I find it distracting while I am trying to drive. I took a left onto James Street, which was kind of a short street. The houses on this street, which there aren't a lot of, are incredibly old; they were built in the forties and the fifties. I drove up the street, and the street was so short that if you blinked your eyes, you wouldn't even think the street even existed; then I turned right on Long Street.

Long Street was given this name for one reason and one reason only, and that was because it is a long street. When you drive up this street, especially during the winter, you must be incredibly careful because it is one of the most dangerous streets. A lot of people get into accidents, and it has a long and steep hill. I was driving up the street, and when I reached the top, I started to go down the hill. I started to coast very slowly so that way I would not slide over the place and lose control of the car.

As I was driving down the hill, there were houses close to each other. On the right side of the street, there were at least seven or eight houses; on the left, there were about five houses. On the right, in between the sixth and seventh house, was a small street called Jones Street, and if you take that right on the street right before you come to the end of Jones Street, there is a park on the right, which is called Hillside Park, the street that the park is on, is Hillside Road and if

you take a left on Hillside Road, which is Main Street.

I passed Jones Street and continued to the animal shelter, which is on the left. It used to be an animal hospital, but when the vet passed away, the town sold the building to two animal lovers, they were spouses. Yes, they were animal lovers; the shelter was across the way from a restaurant called Lucky's Restaurant. They only served breakfast and lunch, and they were a ridiculously small restaurant. They made money but did not do enough to stay open past two in the afternoon.

I saw a parking spot in the parking lot of the shelter, I pulled into the space and shut the car off. I made sure all the windows were shut, I opened the driver-side door, and I got out of the car, shut the door, and put my keys in my right front pocket.

I looked at the shelter, and it was all brick. The roof was flat. It was a ridiculously small shelter. The animals that usually come here do not last long in the shelter because there is always a loving family that is always in need of a pet, and I was amazed at the size of the place. I was thinking about how much maintenance this place really needs. I always wondered if they had a janitor to clean up the place.

So, I walked towards the red door that had a shelter above it, like an awning above the door to protect it from the rain and the snow. I opened the door, which was hard to open and was made from iron, and it was heavy. You can tell the way I opened it. You can always tell when you open the door if it opens slowly and takes you a while to open it, that is because the door is heavy and made from iron. That normally tells you how heavy it is.

Then I walked in.

CHAPTER 2

When I walked in, I looked around and saw that the shelter was reminding me of the inside of the emergency room of a hospital.

The first thing I noticed when I walked in was the mahogany tiles. They looked brand new. It looked like they were just put down. The floor was so shiny that I could see my reflection on it; it was like walking in a glass mirror.

I could smell the aroma of fresh paint; it smelled like it was just painted. It smelled such a nice smell. The walls were all white. I like the smell of fresh paint.

I went towards the desk to check in, and behind him was a waiting room. There were six tan chairs on the left side, and they were connected by a silver bar. On the right side is another set of tan chairs, which are also connected by a silver bar. In the middle was a rectangular brown table that had different magazines on it, mostly magazines about dogs, cats, and other animals.

On the half-circle desk was a green plant on the right, and on the left was a silver bell; in case there was not an employee of the shelter there, you would ring the bell to get help.

Underneath the bell, it said: RING ME IF YOU NEED ASSISTANCE.

So, I rang the bell, and this wonderful, smiley, and cheerful woman came to greet me. She was wearing plain clothes. She had a long white sleeve shirt on, and she was wearing blue jeans, which had the shirt tucked in her jeans. The jeans were really faded. She had a name badge on the right side of her shirt. It was to the far right on the chest part of her shirt, and it said: JANICE.

She had long, wavy blonde hair, and when she smiled, she had perfect white teeth, and she looked like a movie star.

"Welcome to East Meadow Animal Shelter. My name is Janice, how can I help you?" Janice asked.

I said, "My name is Nicholas Star. I'm here to look at a puppy to possibly adopt, you guys called me."

Janice smiled at me. "Of course, Mr. Star, that was my husband Alex who called you. What I need from you is your license, so I can take a photocopy of it, and I will give you some paperwork to fill out.

I took my black leather wallet out and opened it up. I took out my license, which was on the left side of the wallet, and I handed my license to Janice, she did a quick jerk and walked over to the copy machine, and she made a copy of my license, which took no more than three seconds she came back and gave me back my license. She gave me three sheets of double-sided paper, which were on top of the clipboard she handed to me.

"Mr. Star, could you please fill these papers out? They shouldn't take you that long, and while you are doing that, I will call my husband on the phone to let him know you are here." She said as she handed me the clipboard with the papers.

I smiled, and I was so happy that I was going to meet the puppy. There was nothing more exciting than that. I could not wait to see this puppy. They did not tell me about the puppy, the only thing they told me was that it was extremely cute looking, and I would approve of the puppy.

So, I walked to the waiting room and started to fill out the paperwork for the puppy. It took me no time to fill it out. The first page was all about me. They wanted to make sure that I made enough money to support the dog. They asked for my name and my address; they also wanted to make sure I was not going to abuse the animal. On the other side were my finances and they were interested in how much money I had and what I did for a living. The second and third pages were more about how I agree that if something goes wrong with the dog, I would bring the dog back and have them do the work. The last page was that I agreed to cover any costs upfront. I signed all three pages front and back. Then I put the papers on the brown clipboard, walked up to the desk, and handed the clipboard to Janice. She looked everything over.

"Everything looks okay. I called Alex, and he said he would be out in a moment to introduce you to the puppy. She is extremely cute, and you'll fall in love." She replied."She?" I asked.

Janice said, "Yes, the puppy is a female! Do not worry, she is caught up on all her shots, and she cannot get pregnant. We have had her for a year. She's a year old.I was confused; I did not understand why they had had her for so long. The other thing I was confused about is Janice told me she could not get pregnant.

I said, "Why can't she get pregnant?"

Janice said, "Well, we had her fixed."

I put my right hand on the back of my head and asked another question.

"Isn't she kind of young to get fixed?" I asked. Janice said, "Yes, but if we didn't get her fixed and operate immediately, she would have died, and she was a mess. Her insides were completely damaged due to abuse.""Oh, I see. So, you had her for a year because no one wanted her?" I asked.

"No, we got her when she was only a couple of months old. She went through a lot. I mean, when you find out what happened to her parents, it will make you cry; it was sad. I mean, I cried when I found out what happened, but I'll let Alex tell you." Janice said. "Alex knows you are here, and he'll be right with you. Have a seat in the waiting area, and make yourself at home."

I smiled. "Thank you."

Janice smiled back at me. "You're welcome, Mr. Star."

I turned around and walked to the waiting area. I sat down and sighed. I was waiting patiently in the shelter, and I did not wait long at all when I heard a voice.

"Mr. Star?" The voice said.

I turned around and said, "Yes."

"I hope you weren't waiting too long." The voice said.

I walked up to the tall man with a white lab coat on. He looked like a scientist. He was, like I said, tall, and he had short brown hair, as brown as a crayon that kids use to color in a coloring book. He was wearing a pair of thick black glasses. The frame was your typical sixties fashion. The lens was thicker than the average glass. He was wearing a long white sleeveless shirt, and he had an ugly blue tie. It was ugly as a sin, and I wouldn't be caught dead wearing that tie in public. He was wearing tan slacks and a pair of shiny black shoes. When he walked, he could hear the clapping on the floor. So annoying.

I walked up to him. Yes, I'm Mr. Star."

I shook his hand. "I'm Alex Jones, and you met my wife. Let me show you the puppy that we have." Alex said.

Alex and I were walking through the threshold and took a left through a silver two-door hallway. When we went through the doors, the aroma changed. It smelled awful, it smelled so bad I could hardly stand it, and I could not understand how they could stand the smell. As we were walking, I started to ask him a few questions.

"Mr. Jones, I have a few questions about the puppy. Your wife was telling me there was some trouble with the puppy's parents. So, if you don't mind me, ask what happened to them. I persisted.

Alex knew that I was going to ask this question, and he was ready to answer me. As we were walking, he decided to tell me what happened to them.

"Well, Mr. Star, to be honest, I was expecting you to ask me this question, so let me tell you about what happened to her.

This puppy was born on March 12, 1976, and there was a complaint filed against the owners, and the reason was that someone called the police by saying that they were abusing it, and the parents used to beat them so badly that they died instantly.

But before they died, there was an incident where there were some kids who were walking in the neighborhood. As they were walking, both dogs chased them and attacked them. Luckily, East Meadow Police happened to be doing their rounds around the neighborhood, and the police saw the attacks on the boys, and they had no other choice but to shoot the dogs. Anytime an animal attacks someone or is chasing someone out of aggression, they have no other choice but to shoot the animal.

They saw that the owners had a puppy, and the police arrested the owners for animal cruelty. They brought the puppy to us, and we have had her since 1976, but do not worry; she has all her shots. She can't get pregnant, and she won't go into heat."

I started to cry, that was the saddest story I had ever heard, but I could not wait to see her. I have no idea what she looks like, they did not show pictures of her, and I wanted to see her firsthand.

"Well, we are here." Alex said. "I hope the story I told you about what happened to her parents won't discourage taking her home with you. She is a genuinely nice pet, and we have never had a problem with her anyway. Do you have kids?"

I said, "No, I don't. I'm not even married. But my friends have kids, and they come over all the time. I always have parties and stuff like that during the warmer months. I have cookouts, and a lot of people show up for them. I have a big house that was left to me, and I have a big yard, and it's all fenced in, so she won't be able to get out of the yard.

Alex said, "Okay, that is great to hear. She is going to love you. I will tell you another thing, she loves children, and she will be so excited to see you. It has been a while since anyone has seen her or has had company. There is one more thing I really must tell you that I think we should discuss before I introduce you to her. It has given some families second thoughts about adopting her."

I said, "What's that?"

When she first came here, the janitor who cleans up after we close, told us that she can hold a conversation and understand what we are saying. At first, when we heard this, we did not believe it. We thought the janitor was a little crazy." Alex said.

It took me a second to understand what he was saying. I thought he was crazy at first. There would be no way I would be able to tell my friends that she says there wouldn't be anyone in the world that would believe me. I am having a tough time understanding it myself.

When we came to the door where the shelter was, I forgot to mention what the hallway looked like, so here it goes: it was a long hallway, and it was all white, not painted. It was all ceramic tiles on the wall on both sides, and the tiles were all white. The door was a big, heavy grey door that said: ANIMAL SHELTER.

"My goodness, what a story. I do not believe people would do that to animals. I never understood that, nor would ever let me see her." I spoke.

"Well, we are here." Alex said a second time.

Alex felt he was a broken record because he had to tell us twice that we were at the animal shelter. So, Alex and I went through the door, and when I walked in, I saw cages everywhere. On the left were grey cages for cats, and they were all empty and cleaned out, as well as for dogs and puppies. On each side of the room were two shelves of cages. I was in awe and could not believe how clean it was.

Most shelters that house animals have this smell of cat danger, and dogs have this odor if they are not washed thoroughly, but in this case, this shelter takes care of their animals. If animals needed to be washed, they would wash them. If they needed to cut their hair, well, not cats but dogs, they give them a haircut. I was amazed at how well it was taken care of, and as I was walking by, I saw a puppy.

CHAPTER 3

I knelt, and I saw this cute puppy. She walked over to me, and she started to whimper, and she wagged her tail. She was so happy to see me. She was on her hind legs, and she started to bark. Then she barked again, and she was happy.

I looked at Alex. "Let her out. I want a few minutes with her so she can get to know me. Wow, look at her color."

So, Alex unlocked the cage and let her out. She walked over to me and started sniffing my leg. She put both of her paws on both of my legs and looked at me. She was white and brown all over. She had a big black eye, and a black nose. It was as black as a reindeer's nose. She has grown a lot of hair, and every two weeks, she must get her fur cut because her hair grows very quickly.

I sat down, and I called the puppy to come over to me, and Alex was watching. The pup walked over and showed that she wanted me to take her home with me, and I pointed at my face. She climbed up on me; she had a little trouble, but after a while, she got up and started to lick my face. She had a huge tongue, and she wouldn't stop licking my face.

I started to laugh; she was making me happy, and she was tickling my face. I knew right there that I wanted her.

"She appears to approve of you, Mr. Star, and she likes you. She knows you are going to take care of her and not let her down." Alex said.

"Does she have a name?" I asked.

"No, she doesn't. It's up to you to think about her name." Alex said.

"I'm going to think of an easy name that everyone will be able to remember. Finnegan. That's perfect Finnegan." I spoke.

I looked at her, and she looked at me. "How do you feel about that, Finnegan? Do you like that name?"

Finnegan barked. She wagged her tail and put her left paw on my right leg.

"Hey, who are you? You gave me a name, but you didn't tell me yours?" Finnegan.

I was astounded, and I could not believe my ears, a talking dog. Did you talk, or am I going crazy?"

Finnegan said, "No, you're not going crazy. I am talking to you. Come sit down with me, and I'll tell you how I am able to talk to you. Tell Alex to leave, please."

I looked at Alex and stared him down. He knew what that look meant. He knew I wanted to be alone with Finnegan.

"Don't say another word. I'll wait in the hall, and when you're ready, I'll come in. I'll leave you two alone." Alex said.

Alex left the room, opened the door, closed it behind him, and patiently waited out in the hallway. I sat down, and Finnegan sat across from me. I know it sounds crazy; I would not believe it myself. But when Finnegan talked, she talked like you and me. She talked with her top and bottom mouth moving side by side.

I said, "Okay, Finnegan, my name is Nicholas Star. I am a children's author. I live ten minutes up the street from here, and I drive a nice car. I have a big house with a big backyard that I am sure you will love. I have a deck in the back as well. I have parties, and the people who come over to the parties have children, and it was brought to my attention that you love children. Now Alex told me about where you came from and what happened to your parents.

The first thing I want to tell you is that I am deeply sorry for what happened to them. It was also brought to my attention by Alex, that their earlier owners were very abusive and that they used to beat them. One day, there were a couple of kids walking in the neighborhood, and your mother and father chased and attacked them, and they bit them surprisingly well.

If the police did not show up when they did, those boys would be dead. The police had arrested them for animal cruelty, and when they rescued you, they brought you here. You have been here for a year, and not a lot of folks took too well with a talking dog. But I think that's cool. It's fine with me, Finnegan. You have nothing to worry about, and I'll make sure you're well taken care of."

Finnegan said, "Well, Nick, since you were nice enough to tell me a little something about you. I think it's time I told you about myself. In retrospect, you already know what happened to me. You know what happened to my parents and how I came to this place. I appreciate the sympathy that you show towards my parents, and I really do not know why people abuse animals, and then they get upset when animals and dogs attack people. The people that do not deserve it, like those kids, were just in the wrong place at the wrong time.

When it came to my parents, certain clothes, or certain high-pitched voices, it really angered them. I am not excusing my parents for what they did, but what I am saying is that usually, when dogs attack other people, they think might hurt them, which is a defensive mechanism.

"Finnegan, there's a few things I need to know," I asked.

Finnegan wagged her tail. "What's that?"

I said, "Well, I need to know more about how the original

owners treated your parents and how they were abused. How did these people get your parents, and, to be honest, what led them to do what they did? So, I need to know like a back story on them, their names, and that sort of thing."

Finnegan said, "Well, Nick, let me tell you what happened. So, the couple's names are Molly and Jack Stewart. They were the ugliest couple in the entire world. The worst part is they were fat, and when I say fat, they were fat. They make the fat lady who sings look skinny. Their faces were deformed; they were so scary that they had moles and scars all over them. They looked like craters that you see on the moon. But uglier. They did not deserve to have kids. Nor did they deserve to have pets. But anyhow, they decided to have two dogs.

They both were the same breed, and they were both the same color. But the only difference between these dogs was, well of course, one was a female, and the other was a male. The names were Carman for the female, and Mikael for the male.

So, Carman was pregnant with me, and Molly and Jack knew they could not abuse Carman because she was pregnant with me. So, they left Mikael, and they beat and tortured that unfortunate thing. They would bring him to underground dog fights, and to be honest, I do not know how they did not get caught.

So, Molly would stay with Carman in case she delivered me. But here is the thing, I am not the only pup in the litter, there were seven of us in the litter at the time we were born. I know that is astonishing, and we were all born on March 12, 1976.

Fast forward a little; when we were born, people would not feed us, and they would not give us anything to drink. So, they kept beating us and beating my parents. Then, there were times that Carman and Mikael would take both dogs to the backyard, and he would have them fight each other. The only thing Molly would do was watch as they tried to kill each other, and she would laugh. Then they would have people come over to their nasty, smelly shack and pay them to watch them fight. After that, the dogs started to get delusional, and they would now attack anything that walked in their path.

So, one day, it was a beautiful day, the sun was shining, and two boys were walking, and both dogs started to attack both boys without warning. They just lunged at them like a drunk driver lunged at someone they were going to fight with. A police car was doing rounds, saw the attack, shot, and killed both dogs instantly. Molly and Jack were arrested for animal cruelty and imprisoned. The police grabbed all seven pups and took us there. I'm the last one to be adopted."

I was amazed at what Finnegan was telling me, and I still did not know a lot about her. I still needed to know how she was able to talk. I did not understand how she could speak. The last time I checked, animals cannot speak. Well, in their own strange way, they could speak; that's why dogs bark. They bark to communicate with each other or tell the owners that there is someone at the door. Other times, when they growl, it is because they are showing anger, and they want you to stay away. It is a warning sign that they do not like what you are doing.

I said, "Finnegan, how are you able to talk?"

Finnegan said, "Well, that's an exceptionally good question, Nick, and I'll be happy to answer that for you. Right before I came here, the previous owners had a little boy, and he was the sweetest kid when I was born. He wished for one of the dogs to speak so that he could have a friend to talk to. This little boy did not have many friends. No one really liked him in the neighborhood; he was always getting bullied, so he figured if he had a dog that could speak and give him advice on what he should do, he would be happy."

I was amazed, I could not believe what was being said to me. I thought I must be going crazy. I was talking to a dog, and the dog was talking back. I mean, I know animals understand humans, but this is ridiculous. Before I made my decision on whether I wanted to take this dog home with me or not, I needed to know a few more things.

"Finnegan, how are you able to talk?" I asked for the second time.

Finnegan moved her head to the left. She wanted to make sure she could hear my question properly.

Finnegan said, "Come again."

I said, "How are you able to talk?"

Hennegan said, "Oh, okay. When the little boy wished to have a dog that could talk to him, a shooting star flew through the sky as he made the wish. The unfortunate part was, that he would never experience me because when they arrested his parents for animal cruelty, he was a ward of the state. Then, after that, there was a green mist that covered the sky when they brought me out. The carrier I was in was a small, grey container that had a brown handle, and on top, there was a door that locked the cage. On the right and the left of this dog carrier were holes so I could breathe; it was spacious inside. Everyone was in awe when they saw the green mist.

The mist was a thin mist; it was not thick like fog. The color of the mist was a dark green kind of color, and the condensation of the mist is what you see in a horror movie. You could see right through it.

It affected no one; when it slowly came down from the sky, people started to breathe it in, but it had no effect on humans. It lingered in the cage, and I breathed it in, and it started to make me feel funny. I felt like a human. I knew I was fine, but when I came here, I started to make out words, but they could only hear me bark. So, when people hear me talking to them, they cannot make out what I am saying because they only hear me barking. But what I don't understand is why you can hear me instead of barking and how you can understand me?"

I said, "So, I guess you want to know why?"

Finnegan said, "Of course I do."

"So, before I do that, I was a little confused about what you told me about how you were able to talk." I spoke.

Finnegan said, "Okay, sure, what part don't you understand?"

I thought about what I was going to say with my right hand. I started scratching the left side of the back of my head.

"You said that Molly and Jack Stewart didn't have kids, but you mention a child that they had. Tell me what happened with him." I spoke.

Finnegan smirked as she put her right paw over her mouth. She controlled herself.

She said, "Oh, okay, he slipped my mind. I forgot about him. He is not their son."

I was really confused about this point.

Finnegan said, "He's a runaway. Let me explain."

I said, "Please do."

I was sitting next to Finnegan, and she started to tell me about this young man.

"His name is Randall Stewart. That is the name he told them. He is ten years old. When I was born, it was his tenth birthday. His actual name is Kyle Shooter. Molly and Jack told the authorities that he was a runaway, but he really was not. So, Kyle was our typical kid. Jack was coming back from the store, and it was only a five-minute walk from the shack. He saw Kyle, who had a few bags in his hands, and he asked if he could help Jack bring the bags into the shack. So, Kyle told him no problem. So, Jack smiled.

Kyle grabbed the bags and brought Kyle to the shack. Kyle walked in first, and Jack walked behind him. Jack shut the door and locked the door and at first Kyle didn't know what to think or he didn't know what was going on, but Jack told him he was being kidnapped and his new name was Randell Stewart he actually changed everything new birth certificate, new social security card with the name Randell Stewart.

The reason they were not charged with kidnapping is because

they, the police, never knew about it. He was reported missing, but they gave up looking for him and closed his case. He went missing a year before I was born. That is how they got Kyle and why the police did not charge them with kidnapping. The other reason they were not charged with kidnapping was because they could not recognize him because they changed his complete appearance. He was a ward of the state as Randell Stewart, and I hope that answers your questions."

I took a minute to take in what Finnegan was telling me and what she had just told me. I was amazed by the story, and I had to leave what she told me and let it sink in.

"Yes, it does. I have a better understanding now, and I get it." I spoke.

Finnegan said, "Now you know Molly, Jack, and Randell Stewart, how I know them, and what happened to my parents. Now tell me how you can understand the words that are coming out of my mouth and how you do not hear me barking every time I talk. You can hear me talking alongside my barking. That's what I'm confused about."

I said, "No problem, so you ask me why or even how I can understand you and talk to you while you are talking. I think it's time for you to know what I do for a living.

I am a children's author, so basically, I write about animals, whether it be wild animals, dogs, or puppies like yourself. I also write about cats and kittens. My family always told me to come back to the real world and come out of my fantasy world, but the reason is that when I author my books, I really get into my stories, and when I read my books before publication, I can visualize the characters I produce. As I author my books about animals, I can see what animals are saying. Even as a child, I could always imagine what animals were thinking. How the world would be like if we could understand what animals were trying to say? Especially dogs and cats, yes, we know when a dog growls, that means the dog is mad. When a cat hisses at you, it tells you that the cat is mad and does not want to be bothered.

So, I got the idea of writing for kids. I mean, I did try an adult book, but my passion is to write for kids. The adult novel did not do too well. The reason I am stuck with children's books is because I am a kid at heart. I never grew up. So, one day, one of my books started to grow, and the book started to open, I saw the pictures, and it was as if my book were coming alive. I could understand what animals were trying to say. That is why I understand you. Finnegan, I can understand how I understand humans. Does that answer your question?"

Finnegan started to jump up and down, run around, and bark.

Finnegan said, "You are what we call the guardian of the animals. You have a gift."

I smiled.

It was a lot for me to take it all at once, but it was cool to talk to a dog like a human. I got enough information about Finnegan, and I have decided to take her home with me.

I said, "Finnegan, would you like to come home with me? I have a big house and a big yard for you to play in. I would like you to come home with me. What do you think?"

Finnegan said, "That would be great. I would love to come home to live with you. Do you mean it?"

I said, "Of course I mean it. But I thought I would let you know there will be rules you will have to abide by. I realize you are a dog, and accidents happen. But there will be rules we must follow. If you can agree to do that, then I'd love to have you."

Finnegan said, "No problem, Nick."

I said, "Finnegan, you can start calling me dad. I will be your father."

Finnegan agreed. She walked over to me and started to lick my face, and she wagged her tail. She was happy to hear the news. She wanted to show her love for me.

Finnegan said, "Should we let Alex in dad, and you can tell him the good news. I can't wait to get out of here."

I said, "Yes, I'll go knock on the door, and I'm sure he is out in the hallway just waiting for me to knock so he can come in."

I got up and walked over to the door, knocking on the steel door. The noise of my knocking was loud, but it was louder inside the kennel than out in the hallway. Finnegan did not like that sound. The door creaked open. It was Alex.

Alex said, "So, have we decided on what we are going to do?"

I said, "Yes, I'm going to take Finnegan, are there papers I need to fill out before we go?"

Alex was happy with Finnegan; she finally found a home to go to, a loving home. Alex was getting the feeling that I would be a good parent to Finnegan, and I already knew the history behind her. I also understood what she went through. Finnegan was going to be a good fit for me, and I was so happy I met her. The minute I laid eyes on her, I knew she was going to be fine at my house.

I said, "Okay, Alex, I'll take her. What do we have to do so I can own her?"

Alex smiled. "Okay, the first thing I must do is put Finnegan back in her cage just for a moment so we can file the paperwork. Once the paperwork is done, we charge one hundred and twenty dollars, and once that is paid, I will get her for you. I'll make up the tags for her collar, which we make here, and you will get them the same day."

I said, "Sounds like a plan, so let us do this. I want to take her home tonight."

Alex said, "Okay, let's go to the desk and get the paperwork underway."

Chapter 4

I said, "Sounds like a plan, so let's do this."

So, Alex brought Finnegan into the cage and locked the cage.

"I'll get you, girl, in a few minutes, we have some paperwork for your new owner." Alex said.

Finnegan whimpered and put her head down. Alex and I walked out of the kennel and took a right down the long white corridor, and we started to talk about what was going to happen next. As we were talking, I had a lot of things going on in my head. I was thinking about writing a picture book for kids about a new arrival. Alex was a motor mouth, which is when someone talks too much and is not quiet because they want to hear themselves talk. Not my favorite type of person.

Then we went through the double doors and took another right, we were right back where we started. But when I first came to the shelter, I did not know whether I was going to take the puppy, and now I'm glad I am taking the puppy. She is one year old. She was a cute pup, and I could not wait until I got to her home. She will love the backyard, and she will be amazed at how big the house is.

I walked to the desk with Alex, and he asked his wife to start the paperwork on Finnegan and get me all set, so I could take her home.

"Mr. Star, do you know the fee?" asked Janice.

I said, "Yes, I do."

Janice said, "It will be one hundred and twenty dollars, please."

I went into my right front pocket and gave her six twenties, and she counted the money to make sure there was one hundred and twenty dollars for the fee. She handed me some paperwork, which was on a clipboard. "Mr. Star, can you fill out only a couple more pages of paperwork? While you are doing that, I will write you up a receipt for your records."

I grabbed the clipboard and started to fill out the paperwork. As I filled out the paperwork, it was informative; it told me about how to treat animals. It also said that I should have yearly checkups with a vet. I read the information, and I signed on the bottom of the page, which was page one.

I turned the page to the other side, and it had emergency contacts and what the laws in Massachusetts stated in violation of animal cruelty. I carefully read the laws in this state, and I signed and dated them at the bottom left of the document. The last document I had to look at had the shelter card attached to it on the top of the document. It was an agreement that I would make if I could not afford to take care of Finnegan; I would bring her back. I put my name on the top of the document, and below on the bottom, I signed it and dated it. I handed it to Janice; she handed me the receipt for Finnegan.

Janice said, "Thank you, Mr. Star. Why don't you have a seat in the waiting area? I'll see if Finnegan is ready."

I went over to the waiting area, and Janice left the desk and headed to the kennel. When she went through the doors, she saw that Alex had already got Finnegan ready to go to her new home. She had a brown collar around her neck with a red tag that said her name, and on the back were serial numbers and her date of birth. Alex hooked her up. Janice, Alex, and Finnegan were walking down the hall. Finnegan was walking like she was proud, and she should be.

Alex said, "Checking up on me?"

Janice giggled. "I told Mr. Star I checked up on her, and I wanted to tell you he paid his fee, and all his paperwork was in order. He's ready to go."

Alex said, "Excellent."

Alex, Janice, and Finnegan came through the double steel doors, and when Finnegan saw me, she ran to me and started to lick my face. Janice and Alex were happy.

"Hey girl, you ready to go home?" I asked Finnegan.

Finnegan barked, and we started to leave. I shook Alex's hand, and I thanked him for the pup. Finnegan and I walked outside and walked over to my car. She walked over to the driver's side and then walked over to the passenger door. When I opened the door, she jumped into the passenger seat. I started up the car, and she sat on the seat in an upright position, indicating she was ready to go home.

"Ready to go home, girl?" I asked Finnegan.

Finnegan barked. "Take me to my new home daddy. I cannot wait to see it. Big house, big yard, a good owner. We are going to have so much fun together forever, dad."

"You're right, Finnegan. Let us see your new home." I spoke.

So, I backed out backward, turned the wheel to the left on Long Street, and started to go up the hill, and as we were driving, the sun started to come down. This was going to be the start of a beautiful friendship. I thought this would be an enjoyable time to discuss the rules of the house with Finnegan. As I pulled out, another truck was pulling in. It was an old rusty truck, one of those old freezer trucks that they had used back in the fifties. It was blowing black smoke, and the exhaust was shot.

Chapter 5

Molly and Jack Stewart waited for when the coast was clear, and they discussed how they were going to find out where Finnegan was since that's their dog anyway. Molly was at the driver's side, and Jack was in the passenger seat, and they were ready to discuss what they were going to do.

"Jack, how are we going to do this? You know they aren't going to give up that information." Molly said.

Jack thought about it, took his right hand, and scratched his head, thinking about how to answer his wife's question. "Well, Molly, I guess we will have to make them give it to us. No one will realize what is going on, and they won't know who we really are. They are looking for two creepy-looking people, not two gorgeous folks, and we are vampires. We need Finnegan's blood to come out during the day."

So, they knew what they had to do. They were no longer fat and disgusting or looked or smelled like they didn't have the smell of someone who hadn't showered in months. They were clean-cut folks, and they were younger-looking as well.

Jack said, "Let's feed are you ready to suck the blood out of these people?"

Molly said, "Yes, I am."

Molly and Jack wore all black, and they walked into the shelter, came to the desk, and rang the bell. Janice heard the bell first and walked to the front desk.

"Hello, welcome. How may I help you?" she asked.

Jack said, "Hi, I am hoping you can help me and my wife. We were looking for a dog we lost, and we were hoping you could tell us if someone has turned into you guys?"

Molly went around the desk, but Janice didn't see her move; she was quick. She was so quick she locked the two steel doors, the ones that led to the animals that wanted to be adopted. She locked them so that when they drained the blood out of Janice, he could watch her die.

Janice said, "Perhaps you could tell me your little one's name, and I can see if he or she is in our database."

Jack said, "Finnegan."

He took his wallet out and showed Janice a picture of Finnegan, and she saw that it was the same dog that Nicholas Star had adopted.

Janice said, "I don't know how to tell you this, but that dog was just adopted five minutes before you came here."

"Give me the address!" Jack demanded.

"I can't do that." Janice replied.

"Molly, grab her now!" Jack said.

So, Molly grabbed Janice and put her left arm around her neck, applying pressure so the veins in her neck would pop out. At this point, Janice saw her life pass her by.

Molly said, "Now tell us what we want to know, and maybe we will let you live."

Molly did exactly what they said and jotted down the owner and the address it said:

Nicholas Star
66 Nelson Street
East Meadow, Mass 01028

Jack grabbed the paper and put it back in the right-hand pocket of his pants. "Thank you."

Molly's eyes started to turn as red as an apple, and she opened her mouth, and her fangs started to come out. She could see her vein pop up on the right side of her neck, and Molly put her teeth in her neck and placed her lips on Janice's neck, and started to suck the blood out of her. Janice screamed, and Alex heard her cry for help and ran to the front desk, and he saw Janice getting her blood sucked.

Alex said, "Noooo! What are you doing?!"

Jack was behind Alex, grabbed him, and said, "You're mine!"

Jack could move, so Jack bit Alex in the neck and started to suck the blood out of him, and it didn't take long for them to drain the blood out of them, and then Molly and Jack threw the bodies down to the floor like they were nothing.

Molly and Jack left the shelter, went back in their truck, and started to head to Nicholas Star's home to get Finnegan back.

CHAPTER 6

As I was driving, I thought it might be a clever idea to discuss the rules of the house, but I didn't know that Molly and Jack Stewart were hot on our trail. The first reason is it was getting dark. The second reason is that when the sun goes down, it starts to get cold quickly, and the roads start to freeze. That is why I was going slow on the road. So, since I was going slow on the road. So, since I was going slow on the road, this was an enjoyable time to talk to Finnegan about the rules of the house.

I said, "Finnegan, I think I should go over some ground rules and what I expect. Okay?"

Finnegan said, "Sure, let's talk about them."

I said, "Oh, okay, so let's talk then. So, the rules of the house are quite simple. It may take you a little while to get used to the rules because you're used to roaming around on your own. So here they are.

One. First, there will be no going to the bathroom in the house. If you need to go to the bathroom, you either tell me or sit by the door.

Two. There will be no begging for food at the table at any time.

Three. When I feed you in your bowl, there will be no growling of any kind when people walk behind you and try to get around you. Dogs who do that turn aggressive, and they attack. I cannot have that if that happens. I am going to bring you back to the shelter, and I will not tolerate aggressive dogs.

Four. No jumping on the furniture or the table at any time.

Five. Play fighting is fine as long you do not break the skin.

Six. Just be a good girl and a good pet. If someone knocks on the door or rings the doorbell, I ask you to bark to tell me that there is someone at the door.

Seven. No chasing the mail carrier or any other mail carriers.

Eight. No chasing cars, bikes, or anything that moves. Any questions?"

Finnegan was turning her head to both sides, trying to figure out the rules. She was thinking about what I was saying and the rules I laid down. I was hoping she was going to be okay with it. The last thing I wanted to do was get off on the wrong foot with Finnegan. I mean, I just adopted her.

Finnegan said, "I understand, dad. It's okay the rules are fine, and in life, we need rules; that's how the world works. If we didn't have rules, then there would be no order at all. No matter who you are, or what you do in life, when you have a job, you are going to have a boss, and he/she is going to tell you what to do. No matter where you are, there will always be someone to tell you what to do. Yes, you can say you're grown, but in life, you are always going to have someone tell you what to do.

Here are a few examples. If you are renting an apartment or a house or even a space, you will always have a landlord or a landlady telling you what to do, like what he or she wants you to do with the place, meaning a landlord will make rules and the rules are not meant to be broken but to be followed.

Then, if you have a job, you are always going to have

someone you must answer to, no matter if you are an employee, a supervisor, or a manager. There is always someone who will tell you what to do, though."

I said, "People have been telling me what to do for my whole life."

Finnegan said, "Yeah, you write children's books, you are your own boss."

I smirked. "Let me tell you my story and my background.Finnegan said, "I'm all ears."

I said, "So we are only on the top of the hill on Long Street, and I need to glide slowly because the roads are slippery. So, we have plenty of time for me to tell you a little more about me. Finnegan said, "Wow, I'm looking outside of the car, and the snow is even on the trees. It's like a winter wonderland. I've been in the kennel for a year, and I only saw the inside of a cage. I had no idea how pretty it is outside."

I said, "Right around this time of year, when it snows, the snow covers the trees and the ground, and you're right, it makes it a winter wonderland. It's like a whole new world, especially when the season changes."

Finnegan said, "When the season changes?"

Finnegan was confused, she did not understand why the seasons change, so I needed to explain to her when and why the seasons change.

I said, "Yes, we have seasons, so December through March is Winter. March through June is Spring. June through September is summer. September through December is fall or autumn, as most people like to call it.

The seasons change, and when they do, it is like a whole new world. So yes, the seasons are nice and beautiful, but when winter hits, everything is so beautiful. But the only problem with winter is it gets cold outside.

Then, when winter is over, it turns to spring, when the weather changes and it starts to get warmer, and the snow and ice melt. The snow goes away till next winter. Then, during the spring, the grass starts to grow, and the buds on the trees start to bud; in other words, they start to grow leaves on the trees. Then spring turns into summer. When summer hits by this time, there are leaves on the trees, and the grass is greener and grows, but the humidity gets bad in the summer, and it gets so hot that it causes severe thunderstorms, and it rains, which is water from the sky and the thunder gets louder, and the lightning is bright and at times it has electrocuted people and causes damage and even killed people. Then, when summer ends, the leaves start to change color. We call this foliage, and when this happens, it starts to cool down not winter cold but cool. Cool enough to change the color of the leaves. When fall ends, the leaves die and fall off the trees; it also gets very windy in the fall and winter."

Finnegan said, "Oh, okay, I understand that sounds cool. Now, that's informative, but before we go home, tell me more about you."

We were coming down the end of Long Street, and I was ready to take a left onto James Street and I figured it was time to tell Finnegan about me.

I said, "Well, Finnegan, you asked me what I was like?"

Finnegan said, "Yes, I did, dad."

I said, "Well, my life was good. My dad was in service. He served in the Army for four years, and he went to school for music. Then, after he got out of service, he worked for a church for about forty years and retired after forty years. My mom was a children's writer, and she authored books to the very end. When my dad died, it crushed her. His death was really expected. My dad was 90 years old when he died. He died from heart failure. A year later, my mom went to bed and never woke up. She died from a broken heart.

As a child, we always had a dog. We had a German Shepherd, and he lived to be 17 years old. He was a good boy, and when he died, I did not know if I was ever going to get another dog. Six months before my mother died, she stopped writing.

But the reason why I got into writing was that I started to write down a journal and, in the journal, I started to write my deepest thoughts and these thoughts were when my parents died, and I didn't know how to deal with life so I started to realize that I can write, and I should try a novel, and I did. It was an adult novel, a horror novel to boot. It did not do very well. So, I tried to do children's books. So, I started a series of them called Graceville, and they sell like hotcakes. That's my story, and I'm sticking to it."

Finnegan smiled.

I took a left on Nelson Street and drove and pulled into the driveway. Finnegan was astonished when she saw the property.

Right before I shut the car off, a news alert came over the radio. It upset Finnegan.

"Finnegan, what's wrong?" I said as I took my right hand and pet her on the head.

Finnegan said, "It's something I'm afraid of, but I hope it's not true."

I said, "You hope what's not true."

Finnegan said, "Well, dad, I forgot to tell you about the couple Molly and Jack Stewart when they got arrested and that they only got a year. But what I didn't tell you is they were scheduled to be released from jail today."

I said, "Oh, Finnegan, you have nothing to worry about. Believe me when I tell you they have no idea where you are. If they did know where you were, I would not allow them to hurt you.

Finnegan was feeling a little better than I was saying, but when I looked at her, she was still on the kick, sad and worried. Then the news alert comes on:

. . .

"This just in from Channel Seven news. Molly and Jack Stewart were released from jail today. Last year, they were jailed for cruelty to animals and got a sentence of one year in the county. They were not eligible for any type of parole or suitable time due to the seriousness of their crime. They were just released today. If you have puppies, keep them safe even though they paid their debt to society; the authorities are warning people that they are still dangerous."

Then, the news alert came off, and they resumed their regular scheduled program.

Finnegan started to bark violently. Finnegan can bark loudly even though she is only a puppy, which is because when the green mist got into her, the mist gave her the ability to be a full-grown dog, and she grew quickly.

Finnegan said, "Dad, what if they find out where I live? What if they try to steal me? Do you have any idea what they will do to me?"

I said, "Finnegan, listen to me. They will not find out where you live. That's because they just got out of jail, and they won't even know where to look. I will do whatever it takes to protect you, and as long as I am alive, no one will harm you. I promise you that I will protect you. You're like my kid, my daughter, and my property. I love you and people who love people and animals, they won't allow anything to happen to them, and if something happens to them, they will do whatever it takes to get them back. So, what I'm telling you, Finnegan, is I will do everything in my power to protect you, and I will not allow anything to happen to you."

Finnegan started to feel better inside, and she felt a tear come down her right eye. She was not sad, she was touched. What I told her touched her heart, and by the looks of it, I do not think anyone had ever told her that before. She looked so cute.

I said, "Awe."

Finnegan said, "Dad, no one has ever said that to me before.

No one has ever shown me that they care. I know I am just a puppy, and I know I am a talking dog. I also know that an average person who would hear me talk would freak out and scare them away.

But you, you're different. You did not freak out or get scared easily instead, you sat down and talked to me, and when I spoke back, you listened. That is all I wanted people to do, listen. That is all I want to be listened to and to be loved.

You showed me love, dad. I appreciate the love you showed me, and I want to say I love you."

I was touched by what Finnegan told me, she made me cry. I was not sad, I was touched. Finnegan touched my heart, and I was glad that I had Finnegan. I feel blessed and am the luckiest man alive. I have a talking dog. Nothing will change my mind.

I signaled with my right-hand command for Finnegan to come closer to me.

Finnegan instantly came towards me and started to lick my face. She kept licking me and licking me. Then Finnegan hugged me.

"I love you, dad." She whispered in my right ear.

I whispered back at her.

We got out of the car and Finnegan walked side by side with me. We walked to the front door. I unlocked it.

Before we walked in, Finnegan had a bad feeling that Molly and Jack Stewart were closer than she had thought. But the funny thing was she was right.

The couple Alex and Janice were dead and still under the desk of the shelter, and Jack and Molly made face masks to look like them. Now they know where Finnegan resides.

Molly and Jack were outside of the shelter and went in their rusty brown truck to the back of the truck. The cab had enough room to steal all the puppies from East Meadow and train them to fight. They got in, backed up the truck, and headed towards Nelson Street.

"Let's get Finnegan back!" Jack said.

Molly said, "Yes, let's get her back and the other puppies. We have the address for Finnegan, but we must regroup and figure a way to get her."

"Nothing will stop us this time," Jack said.

Molly agreed.

Chapter 7

Molly was driving the old rusting truck, and Jack was in the passenger seat. They came up to the house on Nelson Street, and they saw a man and Finnegan walking into the house.

Molly said, "We definitely need to regroup; we need a plan to get this dog."

Jack said, "Okay, perhaps you are right. Let's produce the plan, but we need that dog, and I will stop at nothing to get her."

Molly said, "Why do we need her so bad."

Jack said, "Well, that is because she has the blood, the blood that will allow us to come out during the day, and her blood will give us eternal life, and when we get that dog, nothing and no one will be able to stop us! No one! We need another person to help us. We need a child, so let's circle around the neighborhood and take us a child Finnegan won't be able to resist."

So, Molly drove past Finnegan's new home, and they drove up to the end of Nelson Street. At the corner where Nelson and Woodchuck Street meet, they saw a young man walking onto Nelson.

His name was Wyatt Richards, he was only 13 years old. He

was five feet three inches tall. He was wearing a pair of tight blue jeans with his white tee shirt tucked into his pants. He was wearing a white pair of cheap sneakers, his parents weren't extraordinarily rich. He had brown, nappy hair, it was long and all over the place. He was starting to walk down Nelson Street. Jack hopped in the back of the truck so he could kidnap this kid and put him in a trance so they could steal Finnegan. Molly pulled up to the boy.

Wyatt stopped when he saw the truck approach him. Molly rolled her window down.

"Hey, young man, I'm looking for my puppy, and I thought I may have seen her around these parts." Molly said.

Wyatt wasn't supposed to talk to strangers, but he didn't feel like he was in danger, and he didn't get a strange vibe from Molly.

Wyatt said, "My name is Wyatt Richards, and no, I didn't see your pup. But you know Nicholas Star doesn't live too far from here. I was told he just got a pup from the animal shelter."

Molly knew she was on the right track, and Jack was starting to form into a vampire. He now has his victim, and he will help them steal Finnegan.

Molly said, "Well, gee, you wouldn't hop in my truck and show me where this Nicholas Star lives, would you?"

Wyatt hesitated to do it. He shrugged his shoulders. "Sure, why not."

Molly grinned. "Go to the door on the back of the truck."

Wyatt walked to the back of the truck, and Jack opened the door and let Wyatt in. Once Wyatt was in, he closed the door and locked it from behind him.

Wyatt had a funny feeling, there was something wrong. He felt evil in the truck. But he knew it was too late.

Jack said, "You know this is a kidnapping, so he lunged at Wyatt and gave him a bear hug, he opened his mouth and sunk his teeth into the right side of his neck and sucked his blood, and Wyatt was turning into a vampire quickly.

"You are now my property, and you will help us get this fucking dog!" Jack demanded.

"Turn around, and the house is the second house on the left." Wyatt said.

Jack went to the passenger side and told Molly to turn around, and she did. She drove to the second house which was next to where Finnegan was living. Jack and Molly had the perfect hideaway and the perfect cover. The house was abandoned. They drove back, and they had to make sure Wyatt wasn't exposed to the sun.

Jack put a black blanket over Wyatt, and Molly shut the van off. She opened the driver's side door and shut the door. She walked to the back and opened the doors. Jack picked up Wyatt and walked out of the van, and Molly shut the doors. They walked to the back of the house, and they needed to get in quickly.

Chapter 8

CHAPTER 8

Molly went in front of Jack and Wyatt to open the first door, which led to the back hall of the house, where you would see shoes and jackets hanging. Then, she opened the door, which led to the kitchen. The kitchen was completely emptied, and the entire house was empty. There was a family that lived there.

The kids moved on, but the mother died of cancer, and years later, the husband died. They cleared the house out in a month and were never able to sell the house because they wanted too much money. The town boarded up the house and never looked back.

Once in the house, Jack put Wyatt down on the floor, and Molly closed the door. She knelt in front of Wyatt. Jack took the blanket off him.

Jack looked at Molly. "Molly locks all the doors. Make sure no one else is here; if they are, I pity their soul."

Molly nodded. She left the rather large kitchen through the corridor where there was a front door. She walked over to the door like she was the owner of the house.

Jack looked at Wyatt, he was starting to open his eyes. Wyatt really didn't understand what was going on. But he was going to find out very quickly about what happened to him.

Wyatt shook his head in confusion. "What happened? Where am I?"

As he said that, Wyatt noticed his teeth didn't feel right. He put on his right index finger, and he felt a tooth that was extremely sharp. Sharp enough to penetrate human skin. Now he was really confused.

Jack said, "Do you remember Molly and I pulling up and asking you where Finnegan lives?"

Wyatt said, "Yes, I do remember that she asked me to come to the back of the van, so I did. I remember I walked in, and you gave me a bear hug, and then you did something for me. I don't feel human, and I remember telling you where that dog lives. We are next door to where they live."

Jack said, "So let me explain to you what happened when I gave you a bear hug, I sunk my fangs into your neck, and I was sucking your blood and tainting at the same time. Then, in your weak state, you told me where Finnegan lives. I gave you some of my blood, so you won't get sick.

Wyatt was in shock. He couldn't believe what was happening to him. "I know Nicholas Star very well. I used to do yard work, watch his house, and do everything else that needed to be done."

Jack was impressed. "Wow, that is impressive. So, he trusts you that's good. I turned you into a vampire, but before that happened, I kidnapped you, and now you will belong to me as well. There's nothing you can do about it. Once I put you under my control, you will be my slave forever."

Wyatt didn't like the sound of that. He was starting to feel better. Wyatt got up and started to get angry about what Jack was telling him. What Jack didn't know was that when Wyatt was sucking his blood and when Jack tainted his blood, that made Wyatt stronger.

Wyatt got up on his feet and walked over toward Jack to speak with him.

Wyatt said, "So, tell me why you want Finnegan so badly?"

Jack said, "It's rather simple I want her blood. She holds an immensely powerful blood that can allow us to become walkers of the day. That means the sunlight will never kill us. That's why I want Finnegan so badly. The person that sucks her blood will be stronger than they ever dreamed of."

All of a sudden, Wyatt walked closer to give Jack a hug, and he had Wyatt in his arms. Wyatt rested his head softly on the left side of Jack's head. Wyatt opened his mouth and sunk his sharp fangs into Jack's neck, and started to suck him dry.

Jack was screaming for Molly, but the problem was Molly didn't hear his cries for help. Wyatt forced Jack down to the floor, and now he was sucking every bit of blood in him. As he was drinking Jack's blood, he was turning more into a vampire, and he was getting taller and bigger. Once he sucked Jack dry, he was dead. Wyatt picked up Jack's weightless body outside and put him in the back of the van. Molly heard the door slam. She couldn't see who it was through the windows because they were all boarded up. So, she yelled at Jack.

"Jack! Jack, where are you? You are starting to scare me; you know I hate it when you play games!" Molly yelled.

She was coming down the stairs to tell Jack the house was clear. Instead of hearing Jack's voice, she heard an eerie voice call her name.

Wyatt entered through the kitchen. Molly was already in the hallway that connects the kitchen and the living room. Wyatt walked halfway.

"Molly, I thought I would let you know that Jack is no more. I sucked him dry, and that's what I'm going to do, which means I will have Finnegan all to myself. "Wyatt said.

Molly was starting to get nervous. "You'll never get away

with this. Finnegan is not going to be easy to capture. You need me. Please."

Wyatt showed no mercy in her. He didn't care what she had to say. "Need you? I need you! No, I don't need you bitch!"

Wyatt's eyes started to turn red, and Molly couldn't resist. "You are now under my complete control. You will do whatever I say. Do you understand me? You are now under my control."

Molly started to go into a trance, and now all Wyatt had to do was say any command, and she would obey. Her body was stiff, and she was acting like a robot. She was being brainwashed.

"Come to me." Wyatt demanded.

"Yes, master." Molly said in a robot voice.

Molly started walking and she felt like she was being pulled like a tractor beam. She felt Wyatt was like an alien trying to abduct people. She stopped.

She was in the kitchen, and she only had to walk a little further to get to Wyatt. Wyatt was forcing her to plunge to her death.

"Closer! Closer bitch!" Wyatt demanded again.

Wyatt was getting real fucking annoyed with this bitch. He believes he will need to suck her dry.

"I command you to walk into my arms. I need you to do that now! Do you understand?" Wyatt proclaimed.

"Yes, master, I understand. I will do what you command me to do." Molly said.

Molly walked over, and she got close enough to Wyatt where he could grab her. He took his right hand and grabbed her left hand, he had a powerful grip.

He swung her with his left hand and arm, and he grabbed her from the back. His fingernails started to grow longer very quickly. They grew a few inches, but they were as sharp as nails and sharp enough to penetrate human skin.

His eyes were starting to turn red, red like fire. His face was starting to get wrinkled; he was turning into an old man, and he looked like a monster. His face was so wrinkled up you could see his cheekbones and the veins that flowed through his body. He opened his mouth, and his fangs were noticeable.

"You now belong to me, and now I'm going to suck every last drop of blood that flows through your body, it will give me the power to where I will be almost human, and once I convince Finnegan to give me her blood, I will be full human and once that happens nothing or nobody will be able to stop me. I will have an army." Wyatt said in a devilish voice.

Molly was getting scared a little bit. "Finnegan won't be that easy to get to. You would have to know Nicholas Star; he is Finnegan's owner, and it will never happen."

The trance was starting to wear off her, but it didn't matter Wyatt had her right where he wanted her.

"Actually, I think you're forgetting that I know Nicholas Star very well, and he has a lot of trust in me. I used to do work in his yard, I remember when he lost his parents and how hard it was for him. I was there for him. Do I think it will be easy? It will be like taking candy from a baby." Wyatt said.

Wyatt opened his mouth, and two very sharp fangs grew from the top and two on the bottom. He bit into the left side of Molly's neck, and as he was biting her, he could hear her moan, and as she was moaning, he was sucking her blood supply.

He carefully took her down to the kitchen floor, and he was sucking her blood. The minute Molly hit the kitchen floor, he had enough blood to make him human to get to Finnegan, and then she died. Wyatt stood up and looked up as if he was looking at the sky.

Wyatt dragged Molly's lifeless body and went out the door, he went to the back of the van, opened the door, threw her body into the van, and shut the door.

Meanwhile, next door was Nicholas Star and his dog Finnegan. Finnegan was on the deck, and she saw that Wyatt was disposing of bodies in the back of the truck, he is a vampire.

Finnegan said, "Oh my god, we have a vampire living next door to me. I must warn Nicholas about this. If this vampire finds out the type of blood I have, well, this whole neighborhood and town will all be transformed into vampires. I can't let that happen. Nicholas must know.

Finnegan started to growl and snarl. She started to whimper, and then the whimper turned into a loud bark. The volume of the bark was getting louder and louder. Nicholas was in his study working on his next book. He heard Finnegan barking extremely violently.

Nicholas got up from his desk and walked through the carpeted hallway and through the wide-open kitchen. When he walked out of the door, he took a right and saw Finnegan barking violently. Nicholas looked around but didn't see anyone.

"Come on, girl there's nothing out there; come on in the house and relax."

Nicholas and Finnegan walked into the house. Nicholas went back to working on his book and Finnegan went into the bedroom on the bed, and she took a nap herself.

CHAPTER 9

Nicholas walked into the kitchen with Finnegan. He sat down at the kitchen table. Finnegan sat in front of him. Nicholas was trying to figure out what was wrong with Finnegan, he knew something wasn't right.

The kitchen was decent-sized, there was a wall where the kitchen table was. It was a picture of a man and a woman holding hands, and there was a child, a boy, who was holding the mother's hand. They were walking, and below said: Family Values.

The kitchen table was a square-shaped table with matching chairs, and on the table was a salt and pepper shaker near the wall. It had a plaid black tablecloth with white mats for the plates, and the floor was a dark marble color. Across from the table were two sinks and a silver faucet in the middle, with the hot water on the left side and chilly water on the right side.

On the left side of the sink was a long countertop that was a lime green color, and at the end was the yellow telephone. It was one of the older phones. As a dial phone, you had to push the buttons to dial someone's phone number, and it lit up as well.

Above the counter was a brown stain cabinet that was professionally installed. As you walk towards the sink, about halfway, there is a dishwasher. It's hard to see, and if you are not used to seeing one there, you would miss it. It's all black on the outside. The inside is all white. When you pull the door down, on the other side of the door, it has two slots; one side is for dishwashing detergent, and the other slot is for extra dishwasher fluid to get the dishes nice and clean.

The top shelf and the bottom shelf were all blue, blue like the sky. The top shelf is usually for small plates, utensils, cups, and glasses.

The bottom shelf is for larger dishes, bowls, and larger objects. On the right side of the sink was more countertop, not as long. But big enough.

The countertop was like an octagon; when you look at it, it really looks like an octagon. The wall on that side was nothing fancy, it was a plain white wall.

On the back of the octagon counter was a toaster, and next to the toaster was a bread box. A white bread box that had the word 'BREAD' on the front of the box.

The brown stain cabinets are in a crooked way that was for spices, flour, sugar, etc.

Next to the bread box is a stove. It was one of the old-fashioned ones. It was so old you must light the pilot. It was white and black. It was all white, the only part of the stove that was black was the knobs on the stove, the medal crates that you would have on a stove, back in the day, that is. The other part that is black is the inside of the oven. There is a fan above the stove to suck up the steam, and that is also the same spot where there would be a light. Most people will leave the stove light at night to save on electricity costs. Next to the stove is an all-white refrigerator filled with magnets and sticky notes as reminders.

So, Nicholas was sitting in the first chair he saw. He turned it around so he could listen to Finnegan. Finnegan started to get up on her hind legs, and right before Nicholas's eyes, he was watching the dog he adopted, and this thing was turning almost human.

Nicholas saw the dog start to transform from a dog to a person. She had long blonde hair, an exquisite and perfect clear face, and makeup, which matched her beautiful eyes. Her eyes were to die because when she moved her eyes in one direction, her eyes would change to an assorted color.

She had a red skirt on and those long boots that were healed, but they were boots. She grabbed the chair near where Nicholas was sitting. It looked like her jaw was going to drop, and he was lost for words.

Nicholas said, "I don't understand it. You were a dog, a talking dog, and now you transform into a woman a beautiful woman at that. I'm lost."

The woman said, "I know it's weird. I know it's confusing. So, let me tell you who and what I really am. I promise I'm not here to hurt you. I'm here to warn you about an evil that is right next door to you. He is an immensely powerful person. His name is Wyatt Richards. He was human, and what happened was that he became a vampire."

"Wyatt Richards? Really?" Nicholas said, surprisingly.

The woman said, "Yes, let me let you know my name is really Finnegan. I am what is called a shapeshifter, which means I can transform into anything by just looking at it. Now, do you remember the people who had me before you adopted me from the animal shelter?"

Nicholas said, "Yes, their names were Jack and Molly. From what you told me, they were unbelievably bad people."

Finnegan said, "Correct, well, when that green mist covered the sky, as I told you. Well, when that happened, I turned into a shapeshifter, I have a good heart now, but at one time, I was just a dog. Then, when I breathed the green mist, it turned me into a shapeshifter. But when it comes to Molly and Jack, the mist turned them into something eviler. The mist turned them into vampires. The reason they were so dangerous is because they are the type of vampires that you would never know are vampires because they look like humans. But the worst part is they can walk during the day, and the sunlight doesn't kill them. So, they kidnapped Wyatt Richards and made him a vampire just like them. The reason they are after me is because, if they get my blood, it will make them the most powerful being on Earth, and nothing will be able to stop them. But there is only one tangible way to stop this. Which I don't know."

Nicholas said, "So, who would know what to do? Someone who knows you and Jack and Molly the best."

Finnegan said, "The only place I know is where you adopted me from."

"You mean the animal hospital?" Nicholas replied.

Finnegan said, "Yes. Let me transform back into the dog you saw at that shelter so there is no confusion."

"Okay let's go hop in the car. Let's go." Nicholas said out of excitement.

By the time Nicholas finished his sentence, Finnegan was back in the dog form, as Nicholas remembered her.

Nicholas opened the door; he checked both pockets to make sure he had the car keys. He did, and he opened the door of the kitchen. Finnegan ran outside, down the stairs, and to the car. Nicholas shut the door and locked it. He walked down the stairs and walked to the car.

Nicholas opened the passenger door to let Finnegan in and closed behind her. He then closed the door, walked in front of the car, and walked over to the driver's side. He opened the door, sitting behind the wheel, started the car up, and shut the door. He pulled out of the driveway and headed up Nelson Street. They were on their way back to the animal shelter in town. What they didn't know is they had a tail that they didn't notice.

The rusted van that Molly and Jack used to follow Finnegan and try to take her is the same one they used to kidnap Wyatt Richards and turn him into a Vampire. Wyatt was driving, following them, and was careful not to be seen.

Chapter 10

So, Nicholas and Finnegan were only a few minutes away from the animal shelter but what they did not know was that no one was going to be there. When Nicholas adopted Finnegan, he met Alex and Janice, who were the people who ran and operated the shelter. They knew everything about where Finnegan came from, and Nicholas had to find out from them why the original owners wanted Finnegan so badly.

They were on top of Long Street. As Nicholas was ready to stroll down the steep hill, Finnegan put her left paw on his right leg, indicating that Finnegan needed to get Nicholas's attention. Nicholas pulled over to the right side of the street, put the car in park, and pulled the emergency brake which was above the brake pedal. He turned to his right so he could face her.

"What is it, girl?" Nicholas asked concerned.

"Nicholas, we need to talk about something that concerns me." Finnegan replied.

Nicholas had this strange look where he was a little confused and concerned at the same time, and the reason Nicholas was concerned was that he didn't know if it was going to be good news or sad news, but the tone of voice that Finnegan was using was going to be sad news. All of a sudden, Nicholas's anxiety started to act up, and he felt goosebumps all over his body. It brought him back to when he was a child; every time he felt he was going to get in trouble either with his teachers at school or his parents disciplining him, he would feel butterflies in his stomach, and then he would feel like he had to take a shit. That's how he was feeling right about now.

Meanwhile, there was a car that was exactly like Nicholas's, the same model and everything. Originally, Wyatt was able to turn the old rusted van that he was using when he touched it into anything. He doesn't just have the ability to suck the blood out of people and get stronger, but he is able to turn anything he wants by just simply touching it. The reason why Nicholas never noticed it was that the car had disappeared, but he was actually there, and no one could see him.

Nicholas said, "Okay, Finnegan, what did you want to tell me?"

Finnegan said, "Well, do you remember when you first adopted me?"

Nicholas said, "Yes, I do remember it was the best day of my life."

Finnegan said, "Molly and Jack weren't just ordinary people. As a matter of fact, they weren't even human. I mean, they were at one point in their life. I'm sure they were good people at one time, too. But something happened. I can't tell you what it is, but there was something. They are vampires, and they will do anything to get me."

Nicholas was confused. "Why do they want you?"

Finnegan said, "Because they want my blood. Because if they get my blood, my blood will give them the ability to stay out during the day, and if that happens, nothing will be able to stop them. Their plan is to make a clan of vampires and take over the world."

Nicholas said, "That's not going to happen. I won't allow anyone to take you or harm you. That won't happen."

Finnegan said, "When they realized they couldn't get me, they decided to kidnap a kid. His name is Wyatt Richards; he used to watch your house. But when they kidnapped him, Jack turned him into a vampire, and what Jack didn't know was he was too powerful, so when Jack and Molly brought him into the house, Wyatt was able to get up his strength, and he sucked Jack and Molly dry, and because of it he is able to turn everything invisible, and he will be able to take me and my power so I'm warning you if it happens don't be a hero."

Nicholas said, "If that's what you want, then so be it. I guess it's a chance we will have to take."

Finnegan agreed. Nicholas turned on the car and continued down Long Hill Street, drove to the bottom of the hill, and took a left into the animal shelter. He parked into the parking space in front of the door, and he rolled the window down so Finnegan could get air.

Nicholas said, "I'll be back, girl."

Finnegan barked and licked her top lip. Nicholas opened the driver's side door, got out, and then shut the door. Nicholas opened the door and walked in.

Wyatt made his way and parked right next to Nicholas's car. His car was starting to form, but it was turning back into the old rusty van.

Wyatt put the van in park, and he was going to lure Finnegan into his van. Wyatt opened the driver's side door, came out of the vehicle, and shut it. Wyatt walked over to where Finnegan was sitting.

"Finnegan." Wyatt said in Nicholas's voice.

Finnegan got excited. "Did you find out what was going on?"

Wyatt said, "Yes, I did."

"What happened?" Finnegan asked.

"Nothing out of the ordinary." Wyatt said, but he wasn't sounding like Nicholas anymore.

Finnegan was shocked; she felt she was being tricked. She was right she was being tricked by evil. Wyatt's eyes started to turn all black, and they circled around and around. Finnegan looked at him.

"Oh, Shit!" Finnegan said.

CHAPTER 11

Wyatt said, "Oh Shit is right. Now look into my eyes."

Finnegan said, "What is going on?"

Wyatt said, "I'm taking you, and you will be mine, and we will have a clan. Now look into my eyes."

Finnegan couldn't resist. She looked into his eyes.

"You are now under my control, and you will obey me and do whatever I command." Wyatt commanded.

Wyatt opened the passenger side door, and Finnegan got out. Wyatt shut the door. Finnegan followed him. They went to the back of the van. Wyatt opened the door in the back.

"Get in, Finnegan." Wyatt said.

Finnegan hopped in the back of the truck, and then Wyatt got in the back van and shut the door.

Finnegan said, "I'm yours to command."

Wyatt put his right hand on top of her coat, and suddenly, Finnegan was turning from a dog to a human. Finnegan couldn't understand why she was turning. When the transformation was done, she was a long blonde girl with big tits and a fat ass. She was gorgeous. Wyatt leaned over her and started to sniff her, and he could smell her blood and how sweet it smelled. Finnegan giggled.

Wyatt sat closer to Finnegan, and she had these big, plump lips that he couldn't wait to kiss. So he put his lips on hers, and she opened her mouth, and his mouth opened, and he stuck his tongue in her mouth, and her big, thick, plump tongue was massaging his, and she was enjoying it.

Wyatt slowly pulled away, and he opened his eyes. Finnegan opened her eyes, and they just stared at each other.

Wyatt said, "I need to explain to you what is going on and what is going to happen."

Finnegan said, "Yes, master."

Wyatt said, "This is a kidnapping, and I'm going to sink my teeth into you and suck all the power that's in your blood, and by doing that, I will be unstoppable, and right before you start to faint and die I'll put some of that blood in you, and you will be unstoppable, and we can live like humans, this community will never know what hit them, they will try killing us with garlic, and it won't work because we will be like humans and it won't affect us, then they will try to kill us with holy water and that will not work, crosses won't work because we will be powerful enough to go into Churches. Then, the last thing they will try to do is kill us with sunlight. With your blood, we will be able to turn everyone we want, and we will have a big clan, and nothing will stop us, and once we take over your neighborhood, we will kill everyone that comes to our neighborhood. Do you understand?"

Finnegan said, "Yes, Master, I do."

Wyatt said, "Once I turn you. You will be able to transform into a wolf, the one thing people are petrified of the most, and once you have them cornered, you turn yourself and suck them dry."

Finnegan said, "Of course." Finnegan leaned forward and tilted her head to the left so that way Wyatt could see her vain.

Wyatt smirked. He opened his mouth wide, and his fangs were long and sharp. He lunged at her neck and sunk his teeth in her, and he started to suck her blood, and as he was tasting her blood, he could feel her power making him stronger and stronger Finnegan was moaning.

She said, "Take my power, turn me into a vampire."

She was still under his control, and then she fainted. Her head tilted backward, and the blood was dripping down her neck, he let go, and she had a little life left. He woke her up. She was in and out, but she came to.

"Do you want eternal life?" Wyatt asked.

Finnegan said, "Yes."

So Wyatt took his right thumb, and his nail grew, and he slit his left forearm, and the blood was coming out. She grabbed his arm with both hands, and she started to drink the blood. She was rejuvenating and getting stronger, and then he pulled away.

Wyatt said, "I'm changing your name?"

Finnegan said, "Okay, what will my new name be?"

Wyatt said, "Your name will be Lilith. Lilith is a powerful vampire, and your body will get stronger and build the more blood you drink."

Wyatt got up and opened the back doors, and he walked out. Lilith followed him. He walked to the driver's side, opened the door, got in, and closed the door. Lilith went to the passenger side door, opened the door, and got in. Both doors shut at once. Wyatt started the van.

Wyatt looked at Lilith, and Lilith looked at him. "Nothing will stop us now."

Wyatt started the van, backed up, and went up Long Hill Street. As the van was driving up the hill, the van disappeared without a trace. Lilith and Wyatt were laughing as the van disappeared.

Epilogue

EPILOGUE
____

Nicholas was looking around the animal shelter and saw no form of life anywhere. He saw a lot of blood everywhere behind the reception desk, which told him that no one was there, and he was getting nervous, and his anxiety was going through the roof. He felt there was something off, but he couldn't put his finger on it. Something didn't feel right about all of this.

He walked out of the shelter, and he saw Finnegan wasn't anywhere in sight. He lost her the same way she said would happen. The only thing he knew was to go back home. So he got into his car, drove up Long Hill Street, and headed for home, but what he didn't know was that he was going to have uninvited guests waiting for him.

To be continued...

PROLOGUE

Here is a sneak peak of Michael Veto's new novel

The dark Entity:
Angel of Death

The sequel to the dark entity

The Dark Entity:
Angel of Death

"Valoc? Who's Valoc?" Linda asked.

Tina was aggravated because Valoc was the most dangerous demon and the hardest to defeat.

Tina said, "We must go back to the kitchen table. I need to tell you who Valoc is, what happened to him, how he became a demon, and how he came into our world."

Linda said, "Who cares about the history of this thing?"

Tina said, "We have to know this because we have to know how to defeat him for good, but to know how to defeat him, I have to talk to someone first."

So, Linda was getting discouraged, so she felt it was time for another cigarette. So, she galloped over to the kitchen table, took a cigarette out of her box, put it in her mouth, grabbed her trusty lighter, and lit her cigarette. She looked in her pack and saw she only had one cigarette left. She said, "Oh Shit!"

While she was smoking, Tina walked over to the living room. She went there because she could sense that Michelle was around, and the living room was where she talked about Nicholas, and now, she needed her help again.

Tina closed her eyes, and she could feel her spirit leaving her body. There was a bright light in the room. The light was so bright that it would blind the average person, and Tina could see Michelle walking towards her and sitting down on the floor in Indian style, facing the threshold. Tina walked over and sat down, facing Michelle.

Michelle said, "Hey, Tina, what's going on with my mom? Why aren't you in the kitchen helping my mom with how to get rid of this demon?"

Tina said, "Yes, I understand, Michelle, but I need to tell her about this demon before we can try to stop this demon."

Michelle said, "Tell her. You know enough about this demon, where it came from, and why and how he came into our world."

Tina said, "I hope she can manage this news, and I will try to prepare to get this thing out of her apartment."

Michelle said, "Listen, this is the last thing I am going to tell you. She will be able to manage this; you have done an exceptionally respectable job right now. Don't worry. I'll be there every step of the way. Mom won't be able to see me, but deep down inside, she will know I'm looking after her."

Michelle vanished, and she was gone. Tina got up and walked over to her body, and her spirit went back into her body, and when that happened, the bright light was gone. Tina opened her eyes, turned around, headed over to the kitchen table, and sat down.

Linda said, "So tell me, what the fuck are we dealing with?"

Tina said, "Okay, the name of the demon is Valoc. He is the president of Hell. He is the right-hand demon to Satan, but before that, he was a beautiful angel. He was pure as they come, but then there was Satan, and his name was Lucifer.

Lucifer was at the right of God. Lucifer was the angel of music. The music he made brought other people closer to God and soothed the angels of Heaven,

So, what happened was Lucifer was trying to rule Heaven and overthrow God, but that didn't work, so Michael the Arc threw Lucifer out of Heaven and into the flames of Hell. But before he did that, he grabbed angels in Heaven and forced them down with him, and these angels are called fallen angels. When Lucifer grabbed those angels and dragged them into hell with him. Lucifer became Satan, and Valoc became a demon, and alongside Valoc was Vetis. That's the history of how they became demons. The way Valoc came through this world was through the Ouija board."

TO BE CONTINUED IN...
THE DARK ENTITY: ANGEL OF DEATH

www.ingramcontent.com/pod-product-compliance
Lightning Source LLC
Chambersburg PA
CBHW050801160726
48004CB00002B/660